A
NARRATIVE

OF THE

PROCEEDINGS IN FRANCE,

FOR DISCOVERING AND DETECTING

THE MURDERERS OF THE ENGLISH
GENTLEMEN,

SEPTEMBER 21, 1793, NEAR CALAIS.

WITH

AN ACCOUNT OF THE
CONDEMNATION AND SENTENCE OF JOSEPH
BIZEAU AND PETER LE FEBVRE, TWO NOTORIOUS ROBBERS, WHO WERE THE PRINCIPAL
ACTORS IN THE SAID MURDER, PARTICULARLY IN THE KILLING
MR LOCK.   TOGETHER WITH THEIR DISCOVERY AND MANNER OF PERPETRATING THAT
EXECRABLE MURDER ; AND ALSO LARGE MEMOIRS OF THEIR
BEHAVIOUR DURING THEIR TORTURE AND UPON THE SCAFFOLD ; THEIR IMPEACHING
SEVERAL OTHER CRIMINALS ; AND A BRIEF HISTORY OF THEIR PAST
CRIMES, AS WELL IN COMPANY WITH THEIR FORMER CAPTAIN,
THE FAMOUS CARTOUCH, AS SINCE
HIS EXECUTION.

IN WHICH

IS A GREAT VARIETY OF REMARKABLE INCIDENTS AND SURPRISING
CIRCUMSTANCES NEVER YET MADE PUBLIC.

TRANSLATED FROM THE FRENCH.

LONDON:

PRINTED FOR
J. ROBERTS, IN WARWICK LANE.   MDCCXXIV.

LONDON:

PUBLISHED BY J. CLEMENTS, AT 21 AND 22, IN THE SAME STREET.
MDCCCXLI.

AN ACCOUNT

OF

THE CARTOUCHEANS IN FRANCE.

As the robbery and murder committed in September last, on the persons of four English gentlemen and their servants, near Calais, justly filled the world with a kind of uncommon surprise, so France seemed more than ordinarily touched with it. The whole nation entertained the relation of it with horror, as if, however innocent, it had reflected upon the very name of French, and that it had been a fact so cruel, and so outrageously vile, that nothing like it had ever been committed but in France.

The robbery, had that alone been the case, had been no more than what gentlemen who travel are exposed to the hazard of in all countries; and the government of France is answerable for no more than the ordinary care, which they always take in that kingdom, to preserve travellers from violence, which they ever have used the utmost diligence in; the king constantly punishing offenders, in that case, with the greatest severity.

But such a piece of savage cruelty as this was, in murdering the gentlemen without mercy, after they had peaceably delivered their money into their hands, filled everybody with an inexpressible horror and amazement.

His Royal Highness the Duke of Orleans, besides having received repeated orders from his majesty, who wept when he received an account of the horrid fact,—I say, his Royal Highness the Duke of Orleans, prime minister, testified his detestation of the crime, by his immediate application to a discovery of the murderers.

Letters were, without delay, issued to all the sea-ports, and to all the frontier towns, passages, and outlets from that kingdom into other foreign parts, to stop and examine all suspicious persons, and all that could not give a satisfactory account of themselves; and to detain them till an account was transmitted to court, and orders returned about them. And, in consequence of those letters, abundance of suspicious persons were stopped in several places, as at Lisle in Flanders, at Metz, at Strasburg, &c., some of whom were criminals of different kinds, though not the particular persons who were wanted.

Nor did the Duke of Orleans content himself with this; but farther, to show the ardent desire he had to bring such flagrant villains to exemplary punishment, letters were written in his majesty's name, to the several princes and states bordering on the king's dominions, representing to them the horrid crime, and setting forth the just indignation his majesty had conceived at the cruelty of it, with his resolution, if possible, to punish the offenders with the utmost severity; recommending it to them, with all possible earnestness, to stop all suspicious persons, and especially such as came immediately from France, and to give notice of it to the secretary of state.

These letters were sent to the several courts of Brussels, Nancy in Lorrain, Turin, Liege, and Munster; to the Hague, to Cologne, Geneva, to the Swiss Cantons, and to most of the princes of Germany, bordering on France.

In consequence of these letters also, several persons were stopped and seized at Turin, at Geneva, and at the Duke of Lorrain's court, and elsewhere; among whom, at last, two persons were found, who, by many suspicious circumstances, were judged concerned in this horrid murder and robbery.

Several persons were also taken up at Calais itself, at St Omer, at Dunkirk, and at Lisle; and among these were three more, who were also suspected. Upon the whole, these were all conveyed in chains, that is to say, chained down to the waggons in which they were carried, and brought to the prison of the Conciergerie at Paris.

Nor was this general search after robbers and thieves wholly in vain on other accounts, as well as on account of this affair of the murder; for several gangs of outlaws and robbers being abroad, this severe search separated and dispersed them. Fearing to fall into the hands of justice, they fled some one way, and some another, shunning, as much as possible, the search after one offence, lest they, though not guilty of that particular crime, should fall into the hands of justice; and though by this means many of them did escape, and are reserved, perhaps, to future mischief, their measure being not yet full; yet several persons were apprehended, who, but for this extraordinary search, had escaped, and some, in particular, of Cartouch's troop or gang were brought in from Lisle, of whom I shall have occasion to speak farther.

The officers of justice having examined the

2 D

several prisoners, and the lieutenant of the police particularly aiming, in all his examinations, at the discovery of something about the murder of the five English gentlemen; they all stiffly denied their being any way concerned in it; nor could the torture of two fellows sentenced to the wheel for other robberies, bring any light to the lieutenant in this affair, those fellows not being really concerned in it. So that, in a word, they began to despair of success, not believing that they had yet made any progress in the search of what they aimed at.

But after some time, the said lieutenant of the police, or lieutenant criminel (as he is there called, came to be informed that one of the persons, who was supposed to be murdered, had been carried into the hospital at Calais, and was recovered, though desperately wounded, and was afterwards gone into England. Upon this important advice, the prime minister was applied to (his Royal Highness the Duke of Orleans having died some time before), and leave obtained to send into England, to desire the person, who was servant to one of the murdered gentlemen, might be allowed to come over to Paris, to see and be confronted with the said prisoners; which was readily granted in England, and the Englishman, whose name is Spindelow, came over to Paris accordingly.

When Spindelow arrived, and was showed the persons, for the keeper or gaoler of the Conciergerie was ordered to bring all his prisoners, one by one, before him, without letting any of them know the reason of it; and prudently giving them all occasion to speak something or other, so that he might hear their voices; it was no difficult thing for him to conclude, that they were the murderers of his master, Mr Seabright, as well by their faces (for we do not hear that they were masked when they committed the murder), as by their voices, both which, to be sure, had been so terrible to him when they gave him the wounds, which they thought had despatched him, that the impression was not easily worn out of his memory.

Wherefore Spindelow immediately singled out two of them, and, pointing at them, declared that he believed they were some of the murderers; these two were Joseph Bisséau or Bizeau, and Peter le Febvre. It is said, but how true I know not, that Bizeau, when he had been named by Spindelow, and was afterwards told who that Spindelow was, said to his comrade, in a violent passion, "Voila! nous somme des hommes mort!" "We are all dead men!" Certain it is, they both discovered their surprise when they were told who this Spindelow was, and that one of the men, who they verily believed they had murdered, was recovered, and was come to detect them,—I say, they were not able to conceal their guilt, the horror of the fact was to be seen in their faces, and it was easy to observe, without putting them to the torture, that they were the men.

Upon this their process was made, and the evidence of the Englishman was taken in form, according to the method of criminal process in France. They were frequently interrogated upon the particulars, but still had the impudence to deny it all; at length they were put to the

ordinary question, that is to say, the torture, when they had still the resolution to deny that they knew anything of the matter.

During these proceedings, the lieutenant-general of the police continued his diligence for the farther discovery of this bloody gang; and partly by the confession of other criminals, who were executed for other crimes, and partly by other concurring circumstances which he took hold of, he got the names of several other persons who he had reason to suspect, and especially of some women, who, though not immediately concerned in the murder itself, yet he found reason to believe were privy to it, as a secret, after it was committed, or had been concerned in concealing the murderers, knowing them to be such; and during the time the search was made for them, as before; and by whose means they were supposed to have made their escape, and, perhaps, afterwards, hearing that they were inquired after, made their escape with them.

The names of some of these women are mentioned in the process, and, as we since learn, their persons are since taken, but are reserved in private prisons to be confronted with the rest of the murderers, when they may fall into the hands of justice, as it is not doubted but they will. Some of these names, I say, are mentioned in the process, such as Catharine Moffat, a Scotchwoman, Mary Frances Beausse de Caron, who kept a cabarette, or tavern, at Beauval, and others.

Joseph Bizeau, the first of the two fellows now in examination, carried it for a considerable time with a kind of intrepid resolution, affecting to despise their interrogating him, whether by torture or otherwise, and confidently denied the fact he was charged with, behaving in a most audacious manner.

He did not deny but that he had been acquainted with the famous Cartouch, who he seldom named but with respect, and with the title of Captain, sometimes, perhaps, that of Colonel; greatly commending his courage and gallantry, and the bravery, as he called it, of sustaining the tortures which they put him to; reproaching his comrades that they did not, according to the oath which they had all taken, attempt to rescue and deliver him, though they had fallen in the action, which, as he said, was but a more honourable and easy way of dying than what they were almost sure of obtaining, seeing, as he said, they generally depended on coming all to the wheel at last, as indeed many of them did every day. All these discourses seemed to be made with such an air of desperation, and that he was touched with a mind sufficiently fired with courage for such an attempt; that when he upbraided the followers of Cartouch with having abandoned him, contrary to their solemn engagements, it could not be doubted that he would willingly have attempted it; and, perhaps, had resolved to do so, but was not able to bring the rest of the gang to join with him, though he had offered to lead them.

It was not without an uncommon passion that he discoursed of that matter, and when he entered into the description of the manner how such an attempt was to have been undertaken, it was observable that a kind of rage possessed him, and he was all over inflamed to such a degree as might easily show he had spirit enough for the undertaking, if it had been yet to be done ; and if we may give credit to what is, with assurance, reported of this Bizeau, he was not much behind his great captain in the worst part of his character, affecting also to be made captain after him, which, when he could not obtain, he separated himself from the grand gang, who robbed in the streets of Paris, and on the road to Chalons, and in the forest of Orleans, and taking the more northern and western parts of France for his station, he robbed chiefly in Picardy, in Normandy, and on the frontiers of the Pays Conquis, attended with such a party of bold, desperate fellows like himself, as he found willing to follow him, and with whom he committed many desperate villanies, and among the rest, this horrid attack of the poor English gentlemen, of which we shall speak by itself.

The time of his imprisonment was not so long as that these things could be thus fully drawn from him in his ordinary discourse ; neither did he, as we ever could hear of, make any formal confession in the manner here set down, though it is evident to many that conversed with him, that the whole tenor of his conversation run upon these things, and that his whole confession, taken after the last torture, corresponded with them.

But the following account, being communicated by a person of credit, who assured us that he had several particulars come to his hand of the wicked life of this Joseph Bizeau, which was not yet made public, and might be very instructing, if they were left on record, we could not but be of the same opinion, and have, therefore, taken out such parts as we found most likely to be acceptable to the world, the whole being too long, even for a book of twice the extent of this short tract ; we have, I say, taken out some part of that large account to add to what we have from other hands.

He says that this Joseph Bizeau acknowledged he had used the trade long before Cartouch was heard of ; that the said Cartouch was at first but an underling, a poor low-priced street-runner, a kind of a shop-lifter, or pick-pocket, and knew nothing of the matter, being only a disbanded foot-soldier, naked, and almost starved, when, merely for his bold, audacious spirit, he was taken in, upon his humble petition, into the great society of gentlemen, as he called them, meaning the gang of highway robbers, who acted in a higher sphere of thievery, and had, for some years, plied the forest of Orleans, the great road to Italy, and the woods about Fontainbleau, where they robbed with security, as well as success, and were seldom attacked, and never overcome.

He says he reflected upon Cartouch, for, as he called it, forsaking that happy gang, his mind still hankering after his old trade of petty larceny, or little thieving in the streets of Paris, where, however, he having seen the manner of the gentlemen of the road, formed a new gang in his own way, and, in time, made himself master or captain over them, and with whom he committed a great many horrid murders, in which they were generally obliged, not only to kill those they robbed, but to mangle and cut in pieces the bodies of those they killed, so that they might not be known, and many times to throw the pieces or limbs of them into the Seine, that they might drive down the stream below the city, and then they were seldom heard of.

This trade, he says, Cartouch and his wretched gang followed in Paris for something more than three years, during which time the city was a constant scene of blood and rapine, no man was safe in going abroad after candle-light, and, especially, no man was safe that received any considerable sum of money at the house or shop of any banquier (that is, merchant) or goldsmith, which is, in English, banker; for he was sure to be watched and followed ; then, if they had no opportunity to attack the persons in that street, while the money was about them, the house it was carried to was so strictly watched that they were sure it could not be carried out again, and then they failed not to find ways and means to get into it at night ; and it was very seldom, if they once got sight of a sum of money in the day, but they found one way or other to come at it in the night.

All things, says our author, have their meridian, their ascension, and their declinations. Cartouch and his gang began to grow rich and formidable by the great success they met with, for they made prizes of exceeding value, even to the tune of fifty thousand livres, nay, a hundred thousand livres at a time ; this raised and increased the fame of their management to such a degree, that at length, in short, the gentlemen in the forest mentioned above began to think of going all to Paris, to join themselves to Cartouch, and so make one body.

The thing was soon concluded, and a treaty or league, offensive and defensive, was made between them, so the out-lying troop came all to Paris ; but, adds our author, Cartouch would never yield that they should quite lay down the road-practice, as he called it, for that, besides the city, they should often have intelligence of good purchase to be made by those who plied in the country. He also thought it might be of service to their common interest to have always a strong cavalry in their service, and to have thirty or forty good horses at command for any emergency that might offer.

This, says our author, I understand was Monsieur Bizeau's province for some time ; and in this time they attacked two coaches in the road from Orleans to Fontainbleau, though attended by a retinue of fourteen gentlemen on horseback, among whom were three of the gendarmes, with their whole mounting and arms, who yet they attacked with such vigour that, after a short but bloody dispute, the fourteen gentlemen were obliged to yield, two of the gendarmes being wounded, and two of the gentlemen killed and three wounded, after which it is not to be doubted but the coaches, in which were only the ladies and the treasure, were easily plundered. Here, it seems, they not only took the money, but, having a house of retreat not far off, they drove the coaches thither, leaving the coachmen and postilions bound in the forest with the gentlemen ; and as to the women, it seems they had their pleasure of them all night, when they acted some things with them which decency, says our author, does not permit me to write.

It seems they murdered none of them, though three or four of the ladies, all disconsolate and enraged, protested they had much rather have been killed outright than be treated as they had been. Whether any one believed them or not, says the author, that I did not inquire.

The booty they gained here was, it seems, very considerable; and as the intelligence of it came by express from Monsieur Cartouch at Paris, so, says our author, a proportionable share of it was faithfully reserved for him and his company at Paris, and was, at their better leisure, transmitted thither.

Bizeau, says the same author, received a shot in the side of his neck in that encounter, and a thrust with a sword, which, entering first a thick belt which he had on, only glanced upon his side just above the hip, and did him but little hurt. The shot in his neck had very narrowly missed the jugular arteries, which, if it had cut, might have saved him from the wheel, but his time was not come, nor his wickedness filled up to its height.

They committed several other notorious robberies in the south parts of France after this, as particularly one upon five foreign gentlemen, with their servants, near Pont a Beau Voisin, which is a bridge over a small river at the extremity of the King of France's dominions, and which parts France from Savoy, and is therefore called by the name of Pont a Beau Voisin, or the bridge of good neighbourhood. Here, our author says, Bizeau, having but twelve men in his gang, was hard put to it, for the strangers, being Germans, and very well armed, as also their servants, and well mounted, defended themselves with great bravery, charging three and three in a rank, and not firing till they came up to the teeth of the highwaymen, and then, twice breaking quite through them, wheeling afterwards about to their own body.

At the first charge they made, says he, they dismounted two of the rogues, their horses being killed under them, and wounded two other of the men, and yet received no damage by the fire of the highwaymen; then the second rank of the gentlemen coming up to charge, with the like fierceness and resolution, Bizeau, says our author, found his men began to waver, and looked as if they did not know whether they should run for it or receive the fire, but he, giving a shout or huzza, and firing his fusee first, to encourage them, they took heart, and fought desperately too, in their turns, so that the gentlemen who made the second charge lost one of their number, and could not break through, as the other had done, which discouraged them, and they were obliged to make their retreat as well as they could.

However, though they were repulsed, they were not yet mastered, but the first rank, who made that bold charge, having again loaded their fusees, they drew up all in a line, with two small intervals, and stood ready to receive the rogues if they came on.

As the highwaymen appeared resolute also, and seemed to be preparing for a bold charge, the gentlemen, considering that it was their money chiefly which the rogues aimed at, and that they had better part with it than run the hazard of their lives, they resolved to parley, and to offer them a sum of money, by way of capitulation, upon which one of the gentlemen advanced a considerable way from the rest, and waving a white handkerchief in his hand, as a sign or flag of truce, desired to speak with one of the highwaymen, calling aloud to them.

Upon this one of the highwaymen came on, but as soon as the gentleman began to talk of delivering a sum of money, the rogue, with disdain, repeating the words—a sum of money! gave the gentleman a curse, and offered to have fired upon him with his fusee.

Unhappily for him, his piece snapping, did not go off, the flint, perhaps, being not good, or from what other cause our author knew not, but upon that insult in breach of the truce, the gentleman fired upon him, and, as our author says, killed him upon the spot.

Bizeau, upon this, advances himself, with a white handkerchief, as the other had done, and seeming not to approve what the other had done, in presenting his piece while under a parley, came nearer, and made signs to the gentleman that he would not offer him any injury, so they revived the parley, and, in a few words, came to an agreement to accept of two hundred pistoles, and the gentlemen to give their parole of honour that they would not cause any pursuit to be made after them in less than three days; so they marched off, after having buried their comrade, as well as they could, and their two dead horses. As to the gentleman who they thought had been killed, he was wounded with a shot in his leg, and another in his arm, but was not dead, and went off with his friends to Grenoble.

Our author tells us of several very bold things done by this Bizeau in the course of his highway war; that his party increased to threescore men, all very well armed, and very well mounted. Among these, he says, they robbed three coaches of the Duke de ——, the Spanish ambassador, though he had a detachment of the King's Guards to attend them; that by a stratagem he found means to have counterfeit orders sent to the commanding officer, to let the coaches go forward with only five troopers, and that he should halt at a certain bridge till the duke himself came up; so joining the party which escorted the duke, that they might be the stronger, till they were past such a wood, where, the order suggested, there had some robbers appeared.

These orders, it seems, he got delivered him, for they were in writing, by a messenger habited exactly as the guards, perhaps, says he, even by one of the troop, who was one of their spies, for they had such in all the regiments which were posted at or near that part of the country.

The officer, says he, entirely deceived, and not dreaming of any forgery, halted as he was directed, and instead of leaving five troopers with the coaches, mistook the figure for a figure of three, as, perhaps, might be designed, and, unluckily, sent but three troopers with the coaches, by which means the coaches were left naked, and were robbed, together with a covered waggon which went with them, in which was great part of the ambassador's plate, and some money, though not so much of the latter as they expected.

During that whole summer, says our author, they robbed in Alsatia, on the frontiers of Germany, and in the country between the Rhine and the Saer, and here they met with very great booty, the German gentlemen flocking into France that year to the Quincampoix fair, as we called it, when the trade of stock-jobbing flourished to such a degree at Paris, as to summon all the gentry of Europe thither to be undone.

While they robbed in Paris all the foreigners that came thither, it was a kind of tacit allowance to Bizeau and his gang to do the like with those they met with going thither, and our author is merry upon that subject, hinting, that those who were robbed of their money before they came to Paris had the better of those who were not robbed till they came thither, for these, says he, lost only what they had about them, but those pawned their estates, drew bills, gave writings obligatory, and entered into a thousand unhappy snares and *faux pas,* to the ruin of their families and fortunes.

Here our author launches out into several particulars, and gives an account of the fate of some good families in Lorrain, others in Alsatia, others in Switzerland and Germany, how they bought up great quantities of the Mississippi stock at vast prices, obliging themselves, by bills accepted, and fatal instruments upon their estates, to pay for them in so many days, all which, in a few months, fell down, by little and little, to nothing at all, to the utter ruin of their estates ; and his account of these are so many, and some of them so tragical, that it is well worth reading, indeed, but as they are too long for this place, and not to our present purpose, we pass them over, and return to the affair in hand, I mean, the farther adventures of this band of plunderers, who ranged over the whole country without control ; for, indeed, the government was so busy, the king so young at that time, and the regent so engaged in other affairs, that no care was taken about things of so small a consequence as a few highwaymen.

But though Bizeau and his comrades had such very good luck, for I think, says our author, they had plundered so many travellers as that they had gotten together six or seven hundred thousand livres in the common stock ; I say, though these banditti had such surprising luck, yet Cartouch and his gang outdid them infinitely, for, as the paper negotiation grew up to such an incredible height that the like had never been heard of in the world, so there was a particular circumstance in that negotiation which exposed people, in a most unaccountable manner, to the depredation of thieves, pickpockets, murderers, and the like ; this our author describes at large, with the nature and reason of it ; we shall only abridge that account, and give it in a few words, thus :—

The Mississippi Company, whose stock rose thus unaccountably high, was (as a company) young in it's business, and not thoroughly established ; new additions, and incorporating clauses and favours being added to it every day, such as the East India trade, the tobacco farm, the debts, the revenue, the bank, &c. ; by this means

no adjustment of stock being made, no books were kept, wherein every subscriber might have had credit for his stock.

Consequently, as the subscribers had no account in the company's books, so neither were the purchasers intituled, by those accounts, to credit for the stock they bought ; in a word, they kept no transfer-book, in which the alienation of the right of every man to the stock which he bought should be seen, or could be proved.

Instead of this, the first subscribers only had tickets, or receipts, or certificates, call them as you will, given them, by which they were intituled to so much stock as those tickets did import ; and as this ticket ran to themselves or the bearer, so the delivering such ticket was all that the seller had to give, and all that the buyer of stock could demand upon payment of his money.

Again, as these receipts had no ear-mark—no number or figures of any kind, other than the day of the month when subscribed, and the quantity of stock they contained, so they could not be particularly known again, or described ; in short, he that had parted with a hundred thousand crowns for stock, had nothing to show for it, or to entitle him to demand it of the company, but these bits of paper, which were the property of the bearer, and of nobody else, so, by consequence, if any man lost his paper, he lost his money, and that irrecoverably ; he could not so much as cry it, nor could any man that found it, were he honestly inclined to restore it, ever know who was the right owner, except by the circumstance of the pocket-book or paper in which it might be wrapped up.

Hence nothing was more frequent, in the middle of the hurries in the Quincampoix street, than to see men running and staring from one to another, confounded, and in a manner distracted, one having lost his pocket, others their letter-cases, others their table-books, with their papers in them ; and whenever such things happened, it was a million to one, odds, that they ever heard of them again.

The sum of the matter is this, that, in a word, this circumstance of the papers was the encouragement of the robbers, and the raising the fame of Cartouch and his company, for now, to get the paper of a stock, was to get the stock, let it amount to what sum soever ; to pick a pocket, and draw out a pocket-book, was to get an estate, and it was a frequent thing to have some gentleman in the crowd whose very pocket-books were worth many millions.

In this work Cartouch was successfully entered, and, if we may believe our author, he had such strange luck, that what with stealing, in this manner, several papers, and the rise or advance of the price upon those papers, while they were in his hand, he was at one certain time master of many millions of livres, in money and paper ; nor did he, like other traders, endeavour to amass a bulky estate in the papers themselves, but after the price was risen to two thousand per cent. he prudently sold off, and turned all into ready money.

And now, could his insatiable thirst of money have known any bounds, he had a happy opportunity in his hand to have withdrawn himself, not out of the wicked trade only, but out of the kingdom of France, and, consequently, out of the reach of justice, and so have lived in a figure infinitely above what he could ever have expected in the world, for he might have carried off above an hundred thousand pounds sterling in specie, and no man that had been injured by him had ever known who had done it, or he ever been in the reach of punishment for his rogueries, at least in this world.

But his fate was irrevocable, and the scaffold and the wheel waited for him, by an appointment that could by no means be diverted, so he went on from wicked to worst, till at length his name became famous, and the world has been filled with his history, of which, for that reason, we shall say no more at this time.

To return to our other captain thief, who was now coming forward apace, and who had, perhaps, been then as famous, had he not been eclipsed only by Cartouch. The fame, as is said above, of Cartouch's success brought almost all Bizeau's troop to desert him, who run away to Quincampoix, in Paris, and, at length, Bizeau himself followed the course of fame, and went thither also.

Till now, says our author, the conduct of Cartouch had been admirably dexterous, subtle, and wary to the last degree, and so well had he managed, that notwithstanding his successes were so many, and his enterprises so great, yet he was never detected; no, not once. Some of his people and dependents were, indeed, catched in the fact, and received their reward; yet so faithful were they to him, or so ignorant of his true name, for he went by several names, that none of them ever accused him, no, not upon the rack; and this caused us to observe, as above, how fair an opportunity he had to have left off the trade, and to have made his retreat from the world, as other wealthy merchants do.

We are now to suppose all his cavalry, as I called them, dismounted, and the road being left free, the whole troop entered into the service of Monsieur Cartouch, and Bizeau himself among the rest; on which occasion our author makes this particular remark: now, says he, the scene altered in Paris, for Cartouch and his followers performed their part by sleight of hand, and, with admirable art, got men's papers, and that, as above, was their money, and the losers were only robbed, that is, perhaps, ruined and undone. But Bizeau and his people understood not that part of the trade; they had no cunning; they knew how to give the muzzle of the pistol in a man's face, and say, Stand and deliver; but they did not know which way to dive into their pockets, and, by true sleight of hand, to whip off a pocket-book or a letter-case.

To make themselves amends for this deficiency, Cartouch supplied them, says our author, with setters and winkers, as the thieves' cant calls them; a sort of people who made it their business to watch the market, and see who sold and who bought the papers—for this was justly called a paper traffic—and to give intimation where they were to be found.

The consequence of this intelligence was, that when a gentleman had sold a paper-stock, as it was called, and received the money, they never lost sight of him till, if possible, they came at the money, whether with blood or without it; for example:

If the gentleman went off with company to a cabarette (tavern), or to any eating-house to dinner, they followed, to be sure, and finding some pretence or other, they would, as soon as it was dark, send for him out into another room, and, making a sham of business, collar him at once, and, stripping him of what he had about him, leave him almost strangled, and unable to call out for some time; so that they were sure to be gone off clear with the booty.

If this was not the case, and it was not found practicable to get him from his company, then they watched him home; and, if it was in the street, they found an opportunity to seize him, whether on the Pont Neuf, the Place des Victoires, or any other convenient place, they chopped in upon him, and then he was sure to be murdered, and, perhaps, to be thrown into the Seine; and many instances were to be found of this part of the practice at that time of day, nor did they ever show any mercy, as we can hear of.

If neither of these were found practicable, then the gentleman, possessed of the money, was followed home to his house, and there he had some chances for his money, which before he had not; and, first, it was then inquired, Whether none of their outlying friends were placed in that house, that is to say, such as were placed as servants, but were spies, to give notice when any booty was brought into such houses, and when it went out, and where; or such as were thrust into houses by sleight, just for the occasion; namely, to open a door, or window, in the night, and let the gang in to rifle the house.

In most, or all these cases, they seldom executed their designs without blood; for the booty they had in pursuit was generally so great, and the method of coming at it was naturally so violent, that there was no remedy but to murder the persons they attacked, and they were, indeed, almost obliged to this butchery by necessity; for that there was too much difficulty in coming at the prize, if the person had life left to struggle for it, or a voice to cry out, which, in a city so populous as that of Paris is, would not fail to bring help instantly about them; they were therefore obliged either immediately to cut the person's throat or to throw a handkerchief about his neck, or, at one blow, to knock him down, and then despatch him, or they would be surrounded with people; and the soldiers, who were appointed, on that extraordinary occasion, to be always patrolling in the streets, would be upon them.

These things made Paris, indeed, be a dismal place to live in; nothing but known poverty was a protection, nothing but broad daylight and the open street a security, so that, after some time, those who were charged with great sums transacted nothing but in private, made no bargains in the Quincampoix but by whisper, and, as it were, in secret, or by appointed retirement to proper places; in a word, a general wariness possessed mankind, and they seemed to be afraid of every one they met; they seemed to take everybody that did but look at them to be a thief, and to clap their hands immediately to the pocket where the letter-case lay, if any man that they did not know came but near them.

It was not, indeed, likely that such a trade as this could hold long. In the middle of their success, the price of their stocks began to fall, and the paper-traffic sunk a-pace, till at last, as we all know, the nature of the thing changed, the shares were all registered, books and offices kept, as in England, to declare the property of things, and this put a full stop to the trade of robbing people of their papers.

In the middle of it all, too, their famous leader Cartouch was taken, and brought to justice, and with him fell the most audacious, fortunate rogue that ever carried on so black a trade. What followed his being apprehended, and how he behaved, what influence it had upon the whole gang, and how he (Cartouch) was prosecuted by the lieutenant of the police; tortured, chained, upon his attempt to escape, and at last broke alive on the wheel; all that part is made public already, nor does it relate to this part of our story.

Cartouch had, indeed, a hardship in the latter part of his time, if our author gives a true judgment of things, as we believe he does, for that his name, by an accident, being discovered by one of his gang who was executed, and that he was the captain of the whole gang; ever after that, whatever great villany was performed, it was constantly placed to his account, and he became notorious for crimes that, indeed, he had no hand in, for after Bizeau and his party came into Paris, they did not only act, as is already observed, by other and different measures than Cartouch had done, but they acted also in particular gangs and companies, neither depending upon nor in concert with him, nor with one another; every one pursuing his own game, and taking in the assistance of any other only as necessity or want of help obliged him to it; nor did they any more share the booty they made, after that, among the whole body; in short, it broke up the society in a great measure, and though Paris was not at all relieved, but was rather fuller of robbers than ever, yet they were not so potent in making great attempts as when they acted in troops, nor, for some time, were there any great robberies committed upon the highway.

However, as is said above, Cartouch had the fame of all, every villany lay at his door, nay, the very society of rogues were called by his name, and are so to this time, for if you would describe a hardened, desperate robber, he is called a Cartouchean; and this not only made him fare the worse when he was taken, but it made his danger the greater, and the government more bent upon taking him, setting a price upon his head, and waylaying him in every corner, so that, after that, he soon fell into the hands of justice, and made his exit as we have heard.

But now, says our author, you are to suppose Cartouch has had the *coup de grace*, and is gone, but the gangs of rogues were so far from being separated, other than as above, or diminished in their numbers, that they rather increased, and though the paper-booties which formerly were made in the Quincampoix street were ceased, yet we still heard of murders and robberies in the streets, breaking up houses, and the like, as much and more than ever.

Fame, busy in new inventions, mustered up new leaders of the troop every day; and for some time after, every thief that was taken was called Cartouch's successor in the command, and had the title of captain; but this, our author assures us, was a vulgar error, and that, after Cartouch, they never had any commander-in-chief or leader, but the whole body separated, and they wandered about in search after purchase as fate and their own vigilance directed.

This, says our author, brings me to a more particular inquiry after the fortunes of Monsieur Bizeau, who in reality ought much more to have been the talk of the world than Cartouch, as well by being a highwayman long before him, as that he continued so much longer.

Cartouch being dead, says our author, and the paper traffic sunk, as is said, Bizeau continued but a short while in Paris, though, while he did stay there, he says, he committed several robberies, particularly taking the Pont Neuf for his station. Here, says he, one night, watching his opportunity, he attacked a certain person of quality in his coach going home, with four flambeaux and a suitable retinue; Bizeau, says he, had twelve stout fellows with him, and first he began by causing an artificial stop in the way by a cart or carriage, of which, they said, one of the wheels was broken, and Bizeau's men seemed to be busy about it, as if they had belonged to the cart; the gentleman's servants intermeddling to make way for their lord, they first picked a quarrel with them, and two or three of them were knocked down in an instant; the next moment, the lord, or whatever he was, found all his four flambeaux were dashed out, and tossed into the Seine, and one of his men with them; that instant, a bold fellow, letting his lordship know he had a pistol in his hand, steps up to the coach, and demands his money and his watch, and assures him, upon immediate delivery, all shall be well, otherwise his men shall be every one tossed over the rails into the Seine, and his honour pass his time not at all to his satisfaction.

This person of quality our author does not name, only calls him the Count de ——, but adds, that he gave them good words, finding what hands he was in, and delivered his gold watch, set with rubies, value six hundred pistoles, and about three hundred pistoles in money, his lordship having had better luck at a gaminghouse that night, from whence they watched him, than he had on the Pont Neuf.

It might be added, that while this was transacting, and to divert the soldiers, who were upon the patrole that night, and had their post in that quarter, another small gang of Bizeau's gentry made a broil of their own in a street hard by, and two of them officiously called off the patrole in great haste, as if there was murder committing in the next street; the soldiers, easily deluded, marched furiously to the place, where they found a great crowd gotten together, but the fray was over, and the rogues had mingled themselves so effectually with the mob, that they were not to be found, so the soldiers went back to the Pont Neuf, just time enough to know—that they came too late.

So easy is it for a gang of artful rogues to

delude the most vigilant eyes in some contrived cases, where the ignorant party has no thought of or guess at the design. Had the commanding officer at that time had presence of mind enough to have marched with a part of his troop, or had he, which was more his proper work, kept his post, and detached a party of his men, to see what was doing in the next street, perhaps he had saved the person of quality from his disaster, and discovered also that he was imposed upon; but the cunning rogues, representing the other fray as a matter of importance, that there was a strong party of Cartoucheans, and that the inhabitants were frighted to the last degree, and begging of them, for the love of G— and the blessed Virgin, to bring the guards immediately; this specious story, and well told also, you will easily grant, might delude any man, and the officer not seeing into it, was not so much blameable for his credulity, as it was called at that time; for, says our author, the officer was severely reprimanded, and not without the intercession of good friends, and perhaps some money also, escaped losing his commission.

Our author's farther account of their adventures contains a great variety of little attempts upon private persons in the streets, and some footpad robberies on the two roads near Paris, most particularly frequented by gentlemen and persons of quality, namely, the road to Versailles, and that to Meudon; but neither of these being frequented as formerly, when the king had his court at the first and the dauphin at the latter, they made no great purchase there, and, in short, their company began to decline apace.

One story our author relates, which seems very particular and diverting, and with which I shall conclude this part of their history. They had observed, or had intelligence by their spies, that a certain young gentleman in Paris frequented two particular houses, both remarkable for the several vices they promoted, viz. one a gaming ordinary, the other a bawdy-house; they had, it seems, a certain account of this gentleman, that if he had bad luck at play he always went away mute and melancholy, and walked directly home to his lodgings, where, 'tis to be supposed, he spent the hours in giving vent to his passions and rage for the loss of his money; but, on the other hand, if he had been winner, and had good luck at play, he went away airy and brisk, humming a song as he went, and his course was always directly to the bawdy-house, where he had a *fille de joie*, as they call them in Paris, who he took a particular pleasure to converse with.

This house was kept, it seems, by an old lady procuress, in English called a bawd, who carried on a very considerable trade that way, and who was, it may be supposed, by what followed, very rich. The gang having observed the gentleman's constant practice, as before, had now no more occasion to set a man to wait above, to know whether he had good or bad luck at play; but they set one to watch his posture when he came out, and if they heard that he came singing down stairs, and called a coach to go towards the Fauxbourg St Germains, for there the lady dwelt, they then knew very well how it had fared with him at play.

It happened one night that this gentleman had had better luck than ordinary, and had won an extraordinary sum, and as his mirth had increased with his money, he came talking all the way down stairs, thus, *trois cent. pistoles, par D——*, adding his oath, that is, three hundred pistoles, by——; and this over and over again, a great many times, and loud enough to be heard, for, till his man brought a coach, he did the same as he stood at the door.

The coach being called, he drove directly to the Fauxbourg St Germains, to the old house, where he used to be merry; but the gang had their notice so early, that truly they were at the house before him, and as they had put on the appearance of gentlemen, three of them were admitted, and had taken up a room next to the place where they knew he usually went; and having gotten two or three ladies with them, they pretended to be very merry, and called for music, and soon after went to dancing, as, perhaps, was the custom.

After some little time, and before their music, in came the gentleman, and, according to his usual trade, had his lady too brought to him into the room where he used to be, and they began to be very merry too.

The lady sung very fine, and she entertained him with a song, and thus matters went on very well for some time, till both parties had been at supper, and after that, as usual, it was supposed the gentleman was treating his lady with a different repast; then the fellows thought it was their time to act, so they bolted into the room just when they were in the height of their enjoyments, and one of them came in singing, *trois cent. pistoles, par D——*, just as the gentleman had taught them.

The young spark, angry and provoked to be surprised in that posture, starts up and flies to his sword, but they were too nimble for him there, and closing in with him, told him they were sorry to interrupt him in his sport, but that they only desired to borrow the three hundred pistoles of him, which he had won of an honest gentleman of their acquaintance, at the Gros Raisins in la Rue de St Dennis, that is, at the Bunch of Grapes in St Dennis's street, and that upon his restoring that sum to them they would leave him and his mistress to go on with their game.

The young gentleman was a man of courage, and began to struggle to get room for his sword; but they soon let him know it was to no purpose, and showing their pistols, as also setting a sword's point to his throat, he submitted, and began to capitulate.

All this while the young Venus lay trembling in the very posture they found her; for though it exposed her to the utmost, being quite undressed, yet they had charged her to lie stock-still, or else they had given their words to cut her open most decently.

In a word, the gentleman pulled out two hundred and fifty of the pistoles, and delivered them, but owned that being indebted to the old matron, the mistress of the house, who often lent him money for his play, he paid her forty pistoles, and that his doxy having not had any part of her usual pension, he had given her the other ten pistoles.

They approved his honesty, they said, and

asked him if the old lady had given him a receipt for them? which he owned she had; "Very well, sir," said one of them, "then you are discharged." Upon this, obliging the gentleman to make no noise in the house, and placing one of their company to see him perform it, the other going into the next room, called for the old lady, who readily coming up, they told her that she must lend them fifty pistoles.

The old matron laughed at them at first, but finding them insist upon it, she then pleaded poverty, and that she had not so much in the world; but they presently convinced her that they knew she had just before received the forty pistoles of the gentleman, and they did not doubt but she could find ten more upon a little search; if not, they told her they would help her look for them.

Then she smelt what they were, and fell a scolding at them, and then to crying, and made as if she would cry out for help; but they let her know also, that she had no more to do but to be quiet or they would burn her house down, and throw her into the fire: so the old bawd submitted too, and brought them the money, though with a great deal of difficulty, and they made her sensible that it was a great favour that they did not go with her and take all they could find. The story is embellished by our author with some lewd pranks they played also with the gentleman's mistress, who they had caused to lie stark naked before them all the while they were plundering him and the matron of their money; but those things, as too gross for our relation, we purposely omit, our business being of a more serious nature.

This story, 'tis said, has many other particulars also, with relation to the fiddlers they had sent for, who they tied neck and heels, and stopped their mouths, so that they could make no music, either base or treble; as also the young whores they had called up for their own use, who they gagged, stripped naked, and tied them to the fiddlers, in a posture not fit to be named. Several other tricks they played also with the old bawd and her maid, which we shall not enter into here; only that they stripped them all stark naked, because they should not follow them into the street and raise a cry after them; swearing to them that if they offered to open a window to cry out, they would shoot them at the window, or come back and cut their throats; as for the gentleman, they used him civilly, but at parting asked his leave to bind him and his mistress together in the same posture they found them in, which, though they might soon untie, yet not soon enough to make any pursuit after them; and in this posture, says our author, they left the whole family.

Had all their depredations been made with such an air of good humour and mirth as this was, there would have been much less to have been said against them; but whatever moved them to the pleasantry of that day's frolic our author does not say; but this is certain, that they carried on their trade of robbery, both before and after, more like savages and butchers than men born among Christians, and, as our author relates things, nothing has ever been acted with so much barbarity and unnatural cruelty in our age.

Few of their robberies in the streets of Paris were committed without murdering the persons before they robbed them, and so many people have of late been murdered in that city, without any discovery of the persons acting in it, that everybody concluded at last, if a man was murdered, the Cartoucheans had done it.

Several of these murders, our author adds, have been confessed at the wheel and on the rack, when the criminal has been just going to execution for other crimes; and most of those penitents have been of the gang of these fellows, who Bizeau had so long been concerned with.

Note; our author says, Bizeau would never suffer himself to be called the captain or leader of these gangs upon any account, remembering the consequence of that vanity in Cartouch; who, had he not affected the style of command, and taken upon himself to be the leader and captain of the whole body, had not been singled out in the confessions of those who came to the scaffold, nor been singled out by the officers of justice, so as to bend their whole application to the apprehending of him.

But Bizeau kept himself concealed by his declining the name and authority of the captain, and yet, perhaps, had as much the direction of things as ever Cartouch himself had.

The turn of things, as I have said, now separated the robbers, and, as is observed, some took to one part of France, and some to another, but Bizeau, of whom we are now writing, chose the north part, viz., the province of Picary, the Isle of France, and the frontiers of the Pays Conquis; this being a part with which, it seems, he had been most acquainted. He had with him his usual number, and which he seldom exceeded, and even these he often divided into two gangs, as we shall see hereafter.

In this new division of the country among them, Bizeau, says our written account, got acquainted with the Le Febvres or Le Fevres, a family or race of rogues, who, as it appears by the same author's account, had lived by the scout, or plunder, for some years; and, particularly, during the late war, the eldest of them, with his father, Jaques le Febvre, were suttlers, it seems, in the French camp, during the several campaigns of the last war in Flanders.

There were, it seems, three brothers of them, John Baptist le Febvre, Lewis le Febvre, and Peter le Febvre; the two former are called vintners, that is to say, in English, victuallers or alehouse-keepers, the latter called himself jeweller, that is also, in English, a cutler or toyman.

This gang of rogues, says he, were rather equal than inferior to Bizeau in their villanies, and had been of fully as long standing in their robberies as he, though of a differing nature, for, as our author says, they were bred up in the army, and yet were not soldiers, but suttlers; that is to say, were, by the nature of their business, thieves and murderers, for those sort of fellows are bred to cruelty and blood, and that in the worst manner of practice in the world, namely, they follow the camp, without any business or employ, as our blackguard boys in England used to do, and whenever any action happens between the armies on either side, or between the detachments or parties, while the soldiers are engaged in the service, and being under command, cannot stir from their ranks, these rogues strip and plunder the dead bodies, and many innocent gentlemen, not only before they are dead, but who, if they did not fall into their merciless hands, would recover of their wounds.

We need not enter farther into a description of this barbarous race of people, or of their bloody employment; it is plain, and known to all who used the army, that as soon as any soldier or officer was wounded, and had fallen, the suttlers, boys and women, such as troop always about and after the camp, would run in upon him like so many vultures at their prey, to hale and strip the clothes off from the dead body, and if they were not quite breathless, they were soon made so by the bloody hands of these wretches.

Nor was their practice upon the enemy only, running in among the thickest of the fighting soldiers, fearless of the shot, which fly as thick as hail, or of the blows, which often light on them, but even the wounded men of their own side were served in the same kind, and that with equal cruelty, if they had the same opportunity; and this made a gentleman, who had reason to be well acquainted with those things, say, that the sutlers' boys and the soldiers' whores destroyed more men than the battle; that the soldiers wounded one another, indeed, but these killed them; for that, wherever they came, there was very rarely any body that was wounded and stripped that ever recovered; nor was any to be found among the wounded that had any breath in them, if the suttlers and the women had been among them.

Of this wretched gang what could be expected but a crew of ruffians, who, being early—from their very childhood—drenched in blood, and hardened against the cries and entreaties of the miserable—deaf to all the most moving expostulations, and strangers to pity and compassion, were ripened up for all manner of cruelty, and the more bloody any undertaking was likely to be, the more suitable to their nature and inclination.

Such this family of the Le Febvre are represented to be by the author above-mentioned; and, indeed, he sets them out as the most wicked, the most terrible, and the vilest crew in the world; abandoned to every thing that was base and horrid; robbers of the worst and most barbarous kind; who yet, by the iniquity of the times, were suffered in the army, where, under pretence of exercising their rapine and cruelty only on the enemy, they were connived at, and remained unpunished, but yet were such as, in the common expectation of mankind, would certainly ripen up to the wheel or the gallows.

It is to the cruel disposition of those murdering brethren that our author lays the brand of the inhuman actions which Bizeau and one of the Le Febvres were executed for; and says that he was assured they were the men that voted in the short consultation they held at the time of the robbery to have them all killed, which Bizeau did not at all think of before. It is true, Bizeau himself does not lay it upon them in his confession, nor was there any occasion for it, because he was not interrogated upon that head, but

we relate it from the same authority, supposing that person to have it from some who inquired farther into the particulars of the tragedy.

With this society, Bizeau, wicked enough before, and bloody too, though now likely to be much worse, kept a close correspondence, and, as they gave each other constant intelligence of everything worth communicating for their mutual advantage, so they often joined their forces together, where the booty, in their view, appeared too strongly guarded for them; and in such case, it was to be observed, says our author, that they very seldom shunned any enterprise for the hazard of it, or baulked a home charge, though they found the persons resolute, and in a good posture to resist.

This character, says he, is more particularly due to Bizeau, for as to Le Febvre, he does not give him the title of a brave man at all, but rather of a base, low-spirited murderer, who had impudence enough to be bloody, but not courage enough to fight; that would murder a man in the dark, and when in his hands, at mercy, but durst not look a man in the face, sword in hand.

In a word, here were two of the worst fellows that God suffered to live, come together in the persons of Joseph Bizeau and Peter le Febvre, and sad was it for the poor gentlemen that afterwards fell into their hands, for the like bloodhounds in human shape were scarce to be found in the world.

We have now a long detail of their wicked actions to describe; we mean, such as they committed after they came together on the frontiers of the French conquered countries, that is to say, in Picardy, Artois, and Hainault, and on the road from Paris to Cambray and Lisle, for these were the parts they plied most in; but we must be content to shorten our account, and leave many of our author's longest stories quite out, as we did before.

One time we find them baulked and disappointed, and that is an evidence, as is said above, that Bizeau was not now matched with such stout fellows as he had with him at the Pont Beau Voisin in Dauphine; that his company now was as bloody, but not as brave; as willing, but not as venturous; in short, that they were rather cruel than bold and stout. The case was this:—

They had intelligence, says our author, of a great booty upon the road between Arras and Amiens, being six gentlemen in a postchaise and a coach, with only two servants to attend them; that there were some Dutch merchants among them, who had accepted bills about them, payable at Paris, for a considerable sum, the bills having been negotiated at Lisle, and fully endorsed; that they had, besides, a good round sum of money with them.

Le Febvre, who, it seems, had first had notice of another booty, which was also very considerable, was gone away directly to Lisle, resolving to lie there ready, so that he might be sure not to fail, and had sent an express to Le Bizeau, who was stationed at Pont Oyse, to advance upon the road to meet him; and Le Bizeau, who had intelligence by another hand of this second prize, had at the same time sent Le Febvre information, and appointed to meet him at a village called Toutencour, on the road from Arras to Amiens, and near the latter ; but they were now so remote that, in a word, they could not think it possible to meet ; so either party prosecuted their several designs upon their own strength.

Le Febvre had only his two brothers and two other men with him, and were but ill horsed neither, being indeed accoutred more like what they were, viz., rogues, than what they endeavoured to look like, namely, gentlemen ; however, he resolved upon the attempt, and as he had learned the exact time when the gentlemen set out, he put himself on the way about two hours before them. The gentlemen he had in his view were only two, the one a commissary's son and the other a merchant, both of Lisle. They travelled in a post-chaise, with two servants on horseback, and the booty which they had about them, and which Le Febvre had notice of, was very considerable, no less, says our author, than two thousand pistoles in gold.

The intelligence which Le Febvre had, both of the money and the persons that had it, was very exact ; but when he came to view them upon the road, he found he was mistaken as to their number, for that being very wary, and knowing the charge they had about them, they had mounted five men more for their security, so that they were no less than seven men well armed, besides the two gentlemen in the chaise, and they had each of them a fusee in the chaise besides their pistols.

Le Febvre had another misfortune too, says our account, namely, that showing himself upon the way, though without any appearance of offering anything to the company, the postman or driver of the post-chaise knew him. Now as who ever knew him, knew him to be a rogue, the fellow gave notice to the gentlemen, letting them know both who he was, and that his character was that of a notorious villain, though they did not know him as a highway robber, for he had but very lately taken up that employment, and was not much known in it at that time.

However, the gentlemen put themselves immediately into a posture of defence, and Le Febvre easily saw there was no good to be done with them without more strength ; so he rode off, not having given them the least reason to suspect that he ever intended anything against them, except what proceeded from his general character, which of itself was such as made all men that knew him expect something or other that was mischievous.

Le Febvre, says our author, went off with secresy, making no show of his design, but rode with all expedition towards St Omer, intending to communicate his circumstances there to another rogue of the gang, who he expected to find there with some attendants, who he knew were always ready for mischief, and who he resolved to take with him to strengthen his company, and so to meet the gentlemen again the next day, he having already had an exact account of the route which they were to go, where they would lie every night, and the like.

When he came to St Omer he found, to his great mortification, that not only the man he came to look for was gone abroad, but that all his party were out with him. He presently concluded it was upon some enterprise of the like nature, and inquiring of a certain female agent, who he knew was always trusted with those secrets, she gave him an account of the message which had been sent from Le Bizeau, and of all the particulars, and how a messenger had been likewise sent to himself on the same account.

In this perplexity he knew not what to do, but calling a short council with his two wicked brothers, they resolved to shift their horses and clothes, that when the gentlemen should see them again they might not be known, and to follow the fellow and his gang to the rendezvous appointed by Bizeau, near Toutencour, as above, and so to get an additional strength there, in order to attack the post-chaise.

As he shifted horses, and rode hard, he was at the rendezvous just time enough to meet his comrade Bizeau, who had the evening before come to the place, and understood that the other gentlemen from Arras were to set out on the next day. This was deemed very lucky by Bizeau, for now they were a strong party or gang of rogues indeed, being seventeen in number, and very well mounted and armed, especially Bizeau and his troop, who came from Pont Oyse.

But Le Febvre had spoiled all their game, for the two gentlemen of Lisle having been alarmed, as I have said, and being apprehensive that, notwithstanding their additional guard, they might be attacked, and that the rogues having had a sight of them, and finding them too strong, might reasonably be supposed to know something of what charge they had about them, and so might, as was indeed the case, be gone away to pick up a reinforcement of their gang ; I say, the gentlemen having been thus alarmed, thought fit to leave the road they were in, which lay to Cambray, and go away to the right, to the city of Arras.

As they might be supposed, when they came to Arras, to be pretty free in their discourse of what they had met with, and what had brought them to that city ; so the news of robbers being upon the road quickly spread over the whole city, and among the rest reached the ears of the gentlemen who were going to Amiens, of whom, as I said above, Bizeau had gotten intelligence, and for whom he now waited at Toutencour, near Amiens, as above.

These gentlemen soon found out the other two, and as their route was not much out of the way, they soon agreed to make all one company. As the first gentlemen had taken five men at Lisle to guard them to Cambray, and who ought now to have been dismissed, they resolved, though it was very expensive, to keep them with them till they came to be out of danger, and by the same just reasoning they prevailed with the six gentlemen of Arras to increase the number of their retinue too, which they did, by hiring eight stout fellows well armed and mounted, to reinforce their guard, so that they now made a body of twenty-five men, seventeen on horseback, and very well mounted and furnished, and eight in the coaches, who were also very well provided with arms.

With all this good company they set out very cheerfully, and besides these they found themselves strengthened in the morning by seven or eight travellers, who fell in with them by the way, to take the benefit of their convoy, though these were not, perhaps, so well provided as the rest, that is to say, not so well armed.

Bizeau was upon the scout early in the morning, and understood his business too well to let them pass him, without doing what he came about, if it had been to be done ; but advancing, on their approach, with only Le Febvre and two more in his company, he was surprised, when, instead of eight men, who he expected, he found a troop of between thirty and forty men appeared, with two post-chaises and one coach and four horses ; twenty of the men riding before in very good order, with one, like an officer, to lead them, and another to bring them up ; and five came behind after the coaches as a reserve.

Bizeau and his comrades retreated upon this appearance, and calling a short council with the rest of the men, they consulted their strength, and what was to be done. He and his own particular gang being bold fellows, and used to charge home, were for venturing and making a bold push of it, alleging the horsemen were not of the king's guards or gensdarmes, but that they were mere bourgeois, that is to say, citizens and shopkeepers, and would not stand; that if they gave them one volley at the corner of the lane, which he showed to be just before them, and then fell in among them sword in hand, they would be put into confusion immediately, and the like. But Le Febvre was against it, and bade him remember Pont Bon Voisin, where he had been very nigh a defeat by an inferior number. It seems Bizeau had told him the story, for Le Febvre was not among them at that time. Bizeau replied that it was true they were a little shocked there, meeting an extraordinary resistance, but that they recovered themselves quickly, and mastered them at last, and that so it would be here, and offered to be one of the twelve of his men who should charge them at the entrance of the lane or defile that was before them, and the other five to dismount and line the hedge, which would, he said, put them all into a surprise, because they would not know the number that were within the hedges.

This he spoke with so much cheerfulness, and backed it so earnestly, with repeating to them what a noble booty there was, that, as our author relates, he had almost won them all over ; but Le Febvre hung back still, and at last positively refused; at which Bizeau upbraided him with want of courage, called him coward, and shook his pistol at him. But it was all one, he would not come into it, adding, that it was an unequal attempt, that he was not in haste to be broke on the wheel, it would come soon enough of itself ; and that they were not troopers, but marauders ; their business was plunder, not blows ; and they might, with a little good conduct, meet with as good purchase with less hazard.

In a word, they could not bring him to make the attempt, and in a few minutes the travellers passed by, the gang lying still in a wood, a little distance from the road ; and thus Bizeau had the mortification to see a good prize slip out of his hands, which, as this account says, he was not used to do ; and had he had his old hardy Cartoucheans with him, he would not have submitted to it, notwithstanding the superiority of their numbers.

This little wrangle, says the fore-mentioned author, parted the two leaders for some time ; and Bizeau, who despised le Febvre for a coward, dropt him, not giving him notice when he heard of any prize, and hardly keeping up a correspondence with him.

In this interval, which lasted above half a year, they committed, says he, many notorious robberies in separate gangs, and not a few murders were also heard of, the latter, more especially, being the work of Le Febvre, who was a mere savage, as I have observed above ; but they are too many to relate here.

The first which this account tells us of, he makes Le Febvre commit in a kind of rage for Bizeau's calling him coward, as if he thought by that method to clear himself of the infamy of cowardice. The story, as our author relates it, is thus :—Going homeward, says he, to St Omer, he met a chaise with two gentlemen in it, who submissively delivered him their money and their watches, which made together no inconsiderable value, and so they went away from them quietly enough ; but on a sudden they returned on the spur ; the chaise-driver seeing them, told the gentlemen they were coming, and added,—" As they have robbed you already, they certainly come back, repenting that they have not killed you, to prevent discovery."

The two gentlemen, not at all surprised, prepared to receive them, and had the good luck to receive their first fire without being hurt ; only the poor driver of the chaise was killed, who gave the gentlemen notice of their coming, and they had only a boy, who belonged to the chaise, to drive it ; so the gentlemen got out of the chaise, and bade the boy drive away as fast as he could, while they shifted for themselves. The boy drove off as they bade him, and the two gentlemen, seeing some enclosed grounds near, made a noble retreat towards the hedges, having not discharged their pieces, which they always presented at the rogues when they approached. At length they got into the enclosures, and then immediately fired at them through the hedge, one at a time, so keeping one shot good, while the other was loading his piece.

The butcherly rogues did not think fit to venture quite up to the hedge, and one of their horses was shot in the little advance they had made ; but that their murdering design might not be quite defeated, they rode after the poor boy, and killed him, who could make no resistance ; and two peasants, or countrymen, who came accidentally by, they fired at, killed one, and wounded the other, as if they resolved to murder all that came near them ; after which they went off, and the two gentlemen escaped to St Omer, which was about two leagues off, where, no doubt, they gave an account of their deliverance, and got some horsemen to pursue them ; but they could not be heard of.

Soon after this there was a house robbed, not far off from Ipres, and all the people murdered in a most barbarous manner, and our author places it all to the account of the same gang, though, as he does not enter into the particulars, we shall not undertake to charge them with it positively, as he does; it was, indeed, very likely to be the work of such a crew, the like of whom we scarce read of in history; and, perhaps, in time a more full discovery of their real guilt may come to light; that is to say, they will go near to make an open confession gradually as they come to the rack, and to be broke alive, which is likely, in time, to be the end of most of them, and has already been of some of the gang in several parts of France and Germany.

But to return to Bizeau and his gang;—they seemed to act in a little higher station than those low-prized rogues just now mentioned; for they kept to the road, except that sometimes they went back to Paris, and did some exploits in the streets there; and, indeed, those were always the most tragical of their actions, for, as is observed before, they generally committed murders there in their street engagements.

But this gang, who sheltered on the frontiers, being, as is observed, the refuse and outcast of the army, the brood of suttlers and blackguard boys, their usage was so bloody that nothing seemed to be attempted by them without it; and, as our author writes, murder was their element, and they delighted in it; nay, even they killed people when no danger of discovery, no difficulty of escape, or any other necessity, pressed them to it.

Our judicious author discants very agreeably upon the reason of this bloody disposition, and next to the cruelty mentioned before, which they are, as it were, brought up in when in the camp; he lays it upon the having always a set of women in their company, and these being by nature timorous and faint-hearted, were, says he, in proportion bloody; and as cowardice is always cruel, so their constant fear of being discovered and apprehended, made them prompt the men to murder and cruelty from that brutish maxim, the dead tell no tales.

At the motion of these furies it was, says our relator, that the very next robbery this Le Febvre committed, they dipped their hands in blood; this was one of the facts which he confessed upon the rack the day immediately before his execution. The story handed down by our author is thus:—

Being at a certain public-house in the parish of Bernaville, in Picardy, where they were entertained in a good hospitable manner, though not as thieves, for the people had, it seems, no knowledge of what they were before they came into the house, Le Febvre began to observe that the woman of the house, or hostess, as they called her, was a widow, that she had good furniture in the house, and some plate, and that possibly she had money also. He communicated his thought to two of his companions, who he appointed to come to the house the night following.

According to appointment, the rest came to the house, and brought two women with them as assistants, and Le Febvre was lodged there that night also, on pretence of buying a horse to proceed on his journey the next day. About midnight, all the family being in bed, Le Febvre rises, and found means to open the gate, and let in his horrid gang, first into the outer court, or yard, and then into the house.

Being come into the yard, they fastened the outer gate again, and went first into the stables, where they found three horses, which they saddled and bridled, to be ready for their escapes; then going into the house, they first broke into the widow's chamber, who they found in bed, and fast asleep; but waking, and in a fright, she began to cry out. They soon brought her to hold her tongue by threatening to cut her throat, and caused her, for fear of her life, to show them where all her plate and money lay, carrying her from one room to another, and torturing her to make her discover it.

In the meantime, the two women assisting them, two of them in another room seized a young man, nephew to the widow, who being the only man that was in the house, they immediately murdered; the woman pressing them to it to prevent noise, and all possibility of discovery. There was a maid and two children in the other room; these the women would have had dispatched also, but one of the ruffians said,—" No, it was enough they would kill the old woman, and he would take care for the wench, that she should not hurt them; and so he did, for he gagged and bound her, so that she could not stir; after which they killed the poor widow too, who, to save her life, had first shown them all the treasure she had, and who had so kindly received and harboured them before.

Having thus murdered the widow and her nephew, and rifled the house, they took the horses to carry them off, and made the best of their way towards St Omer, having first gone four miles a contrary way with the horses, and then turned them loose, that so, if any pursuit should be made after them, it might be guided another way by the horses being found in another road; and this method answered their end, for the hue and cry ran chiefly towards the frontiers of Artois, and upward, the way to Noyon, whereas the gang returned to their haunts near the sea-coast, where we shall hear of them again in a very few days. In the meantime, let us look back to Bizeau, who was upon the wing in another part of the country.

We shall have farther occasion to mention these women in the process of the story, and to give our concurrence to this opinion in the dismal tragedy of our countrymen, the English gentlemen, who were murdered by this horrid crew. In the meantime, their wickedness was not yet come to its full height.

While this coarser and more bloody gang acted, as is said, about French Flanders and the lower part of Picardy, Bizeau and his party kept about Pont Oyse, and between that and Cambray, and sometimes made excursions as far as Rheims and the country of Champaign, and a great deal of mischief they did, even in that well-fortified part of the country, where, notwithstanding the frequent garrison towns which are everywhere interspersed in the country, yet nobody passed in safety, insomuch that the people suspected that the very soldiers who were ordered to guard the roads were the thieves that infested them.

This made the governor of the frontiers the

more diligent in suppressing the thieves, and strong patroles were ordered from town to town, commanded by such officers as might be depended upon for their integrity.

The diligence these men used soon made that part of the country too hot for our marauders, and they began to separate again, and about thirty to thirty-five of them, as was said, made over to England, some of which were pleased to apply themselves to a lawful and regular way of living, and, among the rest of their countrymen, to fall to trade, and manufactures, and improvement, things they had never studied before.

But Bizeau, with a small gang, removing a little into his closer quarters, followed the old traffic, and, by sad improvement, advanced himself to some considerable figure, the profits answering beyond his expectation.

He had not, indeed, taken up a resolution to live and die in the way of his new profession, or that he thought himself hardened against all fear ; but he met with too much success to pretend to leave it off; and our author gives a full account of abundance of his adventures in Champaign, and even in Lorrain itself, and at the capital city of Nancy; among the rest, take the few that follow for a specimen.

He tells us, that being at Metz in Lorrain, a large city upon the Moselle, there were several Jews employed by the commissaries of the French armies to buy up horses for the king's troops; that two of these Jews coming home out of France, where they had been to deliver a great many horses, Bizeau and his gang got information that they were to come back by such a day.

Nay, so exact was their intelligence that they were told the very way they came, and the several sums of money they had received, and which, it was not doubted, they would have about them ; also, that they travelled without any guard, or any other company than three or four servants.

It was true, says our author's account, that the Jew horse coursers had received so much money, and that they were coming back by the road and at the time when the information given said they would come; but the article of the money was missing, for the two Jews had no sooner passed the river Oyse in their way from Paris to Lorrain, but that, having lodged at an inn in a small village near, they were perceived to have money about them, having been observed by, or intelligence being given to, a little gang of rogues, though less acquainted with the trade than Bizeau and his company ; so they had been attacked and robbed just as Bizeau and his crew were coming up to them. Bizeau had just time enough, says our author, to have a sight of the freebooters, and presently knew them, and by certain signals, which those people have to talk with one another by at a distance, let them know who he was ; so they tarried for him, he bidding the rest of his gang to keep the two Jews and their servants safe till he returned.

After a little conference with the other gang, he asked them how much they had got of the Jews ? They told him sixty pistoles and some silver, and generously offered him a share; he laughed at them, and told them they had done their work by halves, and that he would make twice as much of the Jews, or he would search the inside of their hearts for it ; so away he goes back to the Jews, who his gang had carried a little out of the road into a wood, and where they waited his return.

When he came to the Jews he told them he was greatly obliged to them for letting those petty thieves have no more of their money but sixty pistoles, and that they had been so kind to reserve the rest for him; that if they had given all to the other, he should have resented it very much ; but that as he knew they had two hundred and twenty pistoles more in their equipage (and with that he told them to a penny how much they had received, and who they received it of), he would use them, he said, as a gift of so much money obliged him to do, that was to say, very friendly.

One of the Jews seemed to understand him to be speaking ironically, and that he meant by that discourse that he would cut all their throats; and with a seeming resolution told him that it was true they had received so much money, but that he could not blame them for endeavouring to preserve it from the hands they had fallen into; that since he was a man of intelligence, and, as he perceived, had an account of them before they came out of Paris, it was in vain to go about to hide it from him, and he should have the money freely and faithfully delivered; and then he added, that as they had now lost all their money, and had nothing left in this world but misery, it would be no disservice to them to do as he seemed to intend with them, and that to dispatch them out of life would be the kindest thing they could do for them;—at which words the Jew delivered them the money, which he had concealed about his servant's clothes with much art, but with a kind of desperation, and yet an easiness that seemed above any concern, took it all out, here some, and there some, till he *bonâ fide* gave him the whole sum, and then holding out his neck with the same unconcernedness, told him that he was ready for the *coup de grace*, and besought him to dispatch him out of this world.

Nothing could be more moving, says my story, than the manner in which the Jew expressed his sense of his condition, and nothing more intrepid than the spirit with which he called upon the highwaymen to dispatch him.

But Bizeau, as our story sets it out, was really shocked with the poor man's behaviour, and, as he said afterward, says the relator, proposed to his comrades to let the man go, and not to rob him at all,—or to take ten pistoles a man for their present occasion, and so dismiss him ; but he could not persuade the gang to it. However, he told the Jew that he was sorry the loss was like to be so fatal to him ; that he would not have him lose courage,—perhaps he might get it up again. As to them, their trade was for money, and he knew they ran great hazards for it ; that, however, out of his own share, he threw him back twenty pistoles ; and as to his life, he assured him they had no intention to hurt him.

The Jew thanked him, but seemed to lay more value upon the gift of the twenty pistoles than upon that of sparing his life, and so they parted.

And now to follow our relator exactly :—Bizeau, says he, began to draw near the last scene of his villanies. He had some petty adventures, he says, in Lorrain, but not of any great moment, and he was about to retire into France, when he got intelligence of a certain commissary, who, as he was told, was coming from Strasburg in a hired coach, with a strong guard, having a great sum of money with him, some on his own account and some on the king's account; in a word, he had a tempting account of the booty, but withal, he had also such a description of the equipage of the commissary, and that he came so well guarded, that there seemed to be no room for any attempt upon him.

However, Bizeau could not persuade himself to despair, but getting a choice set or gang of his most experienced, tried fellows, seven in number, besides himself and one particular stout comrade, that went always with him, being nine in number, says our relator, they resolved to try what they could make of it, and take what their fortune might present; and, accordingly, on the day when they knew the commissary would be upon the road, they all mounted, and placed themselves in a retreat under a little thicket of trees, where they were perfectly concealed, and yet had a full view of the road.

They had not fixed their ambuscade very long, but they saw some stragglers of the company appear, and those they might have snapped up with ease, but that would not serve their purpose, so they let them all pass, and lay still undiscovered; after some time they saw the commissary with his whole retinue, but were more than surprised when they saw that he had not only eight gentlemen on horseback, besides two coaches, but had also a little squadron of dragoons with him, which the governor of Strasburg had granted because of the king's money, which was also with them, and was a considerable sum.

This sight made them disconsolate, and they had no more to do but lie still till the whole body was passed, and so disposed themselves to return to their homes, or wander about for anything that might offer.

In pursuit of these thoughts, they came into the road, for, as is said, they had taken their standing at a little distance from the highway, that they might lie secure; but now, coming into the road, they rode off the contrary way, going towards Strasburg, that they might not be seen by any of the dragoons.

The first they met with, says our author, were two dragoons following the coach upon the spur, which, it must be supposed, were two of the number appointed to have gone with the rest, but who were left behind by their own negligence; they inquired of Bizeau and his gang if they had seen the party before, which the other told them they had, and that they were but about half a league off; so they parted. Bizeau was at first minded to have attacked them, but he considered that soldiers are not generally overstocked with money, and that if he attempted them, he must kill them both or he did nothing; then also, that perhaps the noise might be heard by the rest, who were not yet a great way before, and might come back to their rescue, so he let them pass.

But he had not rode above half a mile farther, when he met with a coach and six horses, driving also furiously after the rest, as if intending to overtake them, and that either they belonged to them, or were travellers, willing to have the benefit of their convoy.

They had three horsemen, who made up their retinue, but, happily for them, the coach drove so hard that they could not keep pace, and were at least a league behind; had they been with the coach, Bizeau would have found it needful to have killed them, that he might rob the coach without their escaping and raising the country.

The gentlemen in the coach, says our relation, seeing Bizeau, but not the rest of his gang, stopped to inquire after their convoy, and this gave Bizeau opportunity to come close up to them, and as they inquired, so he gave them a particular account how far off they were, not forgetting to suggest that they were a league farther off than they really were.

In this interval two of Bizeau's men were come up to the postilion, and stood close to him, while the other seven stood a little way from them, so that the gentlemen in the coach did not see them. A while after, the gentlemen having, as it were, done talking with Bizeau, bade the coachman go on, and the coachman called to the postilion to move; but in that instant the rest of the gang, as if that had been their signal, came galloping up on each side of the coach, and bidding the coachman stop, gave the word deliver to the gentlemen in the coach; Bizeau, in the meantime, as if he had known nothing of the matter, rode away, so that they never imagined they had called a highwayman to them, or that he belonged to the party.

When the gentlemen found how it was, they would have got out of the coach, but having three horsemen on one side and four on the other, they could not attempt it, and the first thing the gang demanded was to deliver their arms, which they were very unwilling to do; but seeing no remedy, for the highwaymen presented their carbines at them, and told them, if they did not immediately deliver their arms, they were all dead men—we say, seeing there was no remedy, they submitted, to be sure, and gave out their arms.

The gang had no intelligence of this coach, so could not tell what to expect, or where to search more particularly than other, so they obliged the gentlemen to alight out of the coach, and searched them, one by one, so effectually, that they almost stripped them from head to foot.

While this was doing, and after their arms were delivered, three of the gang alighting, searched the coach and the portmanteaus, which were tied behind and before, while Bizeau, with three more, who he called off to him, rode forward towards Strasburg, to scour the road and secure the work.

In their going forward, which, indeed, was wisely contrived, though they knew not of it, they met the gentlemen's three servants, and two other men with them, coming after the coach, as it happened; the two other men were peasants, and so had no arms; and they fell into the same snare their masters had done, for one of them rides up to Bizeau, who was a little before the rest, and asked him if they met a coach and six horses, and how far they were off?

Bizeau, says he, answered yes, he did meet a

2 E

coach, and they were not far off; but, sir, says he, I must speak a word with you before you go after them, and with that presents his carbine at him and bids him stand. The fellow seemed surprised, and having a fuzee slung at his back, began to lay his hand on it, which Bizeau seeing, fired at him immediately, and fetched him off his horse, though, as it proved afterwards, the fellow was not killed, but sore wounded and worse frightened. The other two, seeing what hands they were in, and that there was no room to fly, or pretence to fight with four resolute fellows well armed, submitted; and as for the two peasants, they had neither weapons nor money, so they stood at a small distance, and looked on the highwaymen, who commanded them, on pain of death, not to stir a foot.

The other had not much to lose, being servants; they confessed they belonged to the coach, and when they had been told what had been their masters' fate, they exclaimed at their own negligence at being absent; but Bizeau satisfied them that it was their felicity, and perhaps their masters' too, that they were so absent, for that, if they had been there, they had infallibly been all killed, and perhaps their masters also.

But to go back to the coach; the gang having, as is said, effectually plundered them, they called a council what they should do with them; some of them, it seems, moved to kill the postilion, others the coachman and postilion, and one to kill them all; but it was at length carried for more merciful measures, namely, to cut all the harness and turn the horses loose, then overthrow the coach, and leave them all to take what measures they thought fit.

But the gentlemen, by their importunities, prevailed with them to leave the coach and harness all entire, promising, upon their words and honour, to go all into the coach and sit stockstill four hours, and then drive directly back to Strasburg; and that if any person came by on the road, they would not make any complaint, or discover what had happened to them.

Bizeau was by this time come back to them, and all things being done and finished with the utmost dispatch, the gang, not much afraid of pursuit, and taking a contrary road, left the gentlemen to perform quarantine, pursuant to their parole, which they did very punctually, according to promise; Bizeau and his gang going away towards Landau and the Rhine, where they would soon be beyond the reach of pursuit, being then in the dominions of the emperor.

This is the last considerable adventure which, he says, Bizeau was concerned in, and he seems something uncertain whether he was personally in this adventure or no; or that his immediate comrade, mentioned above, who it seems was his nephew, was rather principal in it, and that Joseph Bizeau might be engaged in some of the other attempts, which take up that part of his relation; so we leave that part as we find it, nor is it very material which of them it was.

The booty the gang made of this rencounter, for such it seemed to be in its circumstances, they having not the least intelligence about it,— we say, the booty was not inconsiderable, the gentlemen, as may be supposed from the equipage they travelled in, being well furnished, and

perhaps the better for being so secure, as they thought themselves, under the convoy of a party of the king's troops; but our author does not enter into the particulars of what they took here, except that he hints their changing a horse with one of the servants, who had a very good one.

As the gang, you see, was great, so you are not to suppose that these were all the adventures that they went about in the space of two years, from the time they came first to Paris to that adventure near Strasburg; nor, as I said above, do we give a full account of those which our relator above-mentioned is stored with, but, as is noted before, have singled out some of the most diverting and the most considerable, for our reader's observation, even as far back as the late peace, when the reduction of the troops in France left a considerable number of gentlemen out of employment, and in want of means to subsist, we say, ever since the late war.

During these adventures of Bizeau and his gang, we are not to suppose Le Febvre and his blackguard gang were idle.

Le Febvre himself had, for some time before, joined himself on several occasions with another gang of highway robbers at Paris, and these kept their station about Chalons, and on the frontiers of Burgundy, where they committed several notorious murders and robberies, for wherever he acted, it seems, he was generally drenched in blood.

It was in conjunction with this gang that he had once robbed the coach called Le Diligence, about two years before, namely, in April, 1721, and also in robbing and murdering one D'Angers, a courier on the road from Paris to Chartres, which murder he confessed also upon the torture. It seems the courier was going for Spain, and, as they supposed, had some rich presents from the Duke of Orleans to the King of Spain on a particular account; so that, without any capitulation, they attacked and murdered him, and rifled him afterwards, when, to their great surprise, they found nothing about him but about twenty-four pistoles to defray his expenses on his journey.

After this, says the same account, they attacked three citizens of Orleans, travelling from that city towards Auxerre, who they robbed of about six hundred livres, and wounding one of them, threw him into the Canal de Briaire, intending to drown him; but as they rode off upon the approach of some peasants, the citizen made his escape.

Then they robbed the coach mentioned above a second time. It was, it seems, upon some intelligence they had of a great booty in the coach that they attacked it this second time, and it was reported that they found no less than seventy thousand livres in money in it, which, however, says our author, wants confirmation. At this last time of robbing the Lyons stage-coach they fired at three horsemen who were with them, and rode for it; it seems one of them was shot in the arm, but they got away, being well mounted; and with them, says he, it was reported they missed a larger booty, two of the gentlemen having a considerable sum of money with them.

At the robbing this coach they committed no

murder; but, says our author, it was not for want of endeavour, but because the gentlemen escaped by the goodness of their horses; for it was otherwise their constant practice, that whenever they attempted to rob a coach, they always murdered the attendants, though they never killed those who were in the coach : it seems they murdered the other, not only that they might not escape and raise the country, but also that they might give them no disturbance during their further operations with the coach.

The escape of those three persons, it seems, made them the more in haste in rifling the coach, where, notwithstanding the seventy thousand livres which it was said they found, yet they left some things of value for want of time to make a more particular search.

This also is one of the robberies which Le Febvre confessed upon the rack, and which the officers who tortured them were particularly directed to question them about.

By these it will sufficiently appear that not only from the time when the famous Cartouch was in his meridian of wickedness, but for some time before, there has been a formidable gang of robbers in France, who, as well on the road in the forest of Orleans and frontiers of Flanders, and other places in the country, as also in the streets of the city of Paris, have carried on the thieving trade and other villanies, complicated with divers horrid murders and insolencies; and this, notwithstanding the utmost vigilance in the proper officers to apprehend them, and the utmost severity in the government to punish them when apprehended ; for not one of them that has been apprehended has been spared, except only such as have been made use of to detect and convict their fellows.

Of this horrid race of men, and thus introduced, these two, whose execution has been so justly severe, and who we are now speaking of, are produced ; and if the author, from whom these facts are thus published, had made a true collection, they have had a great length of time to practise their villanies in, and had a mass of blood to account for to the justice of men, besides what a load of crimes may have been committed by them, which the world as yet knows nothing of.

It is true, the name of Cartouch has borne the burthen of most of these things, I mean as to the scandal of them ; fame has sported with his character, and has placed every action that has been superlatively and flagrantly wicked to his account. But if we come to examine things more nicely, we find the thing quite otherwise, and, for aught that we see, Joseph Bizeau was a bolder and more enterprising villain than he, and Le Febvre a more merciless, bloody, and butcherly rogue than either of them ; and if the detail of all their lives was more fully described, I doubt not but it would appear so in every particular, at least the close of their actions would certainly confirm it.

As is said above, Bizeau was now come to the last scene of his life. While he had, as it were, taken up the north-east parts of France for his station, and that he plied about Lorrain, and the country between the Rhine and Moselle, he received a message from some of his comrades, inviting him, or rather soliciting him, to come into Picardy, upon some intelligence of an extraordinary booty to be made, and a sort of a certainty of making it well worth his while.

What this particular adventure was, or upon what prospect it was proposed, our relator does not particularly give an account, or whether it was effected and brought to pass, or that they met with a disappointment and made no advantage as they expected ; but as it seems to be named chiefly to bring Bizeau into Flanders and Picardy, so it answers the end that way, for now we read of him always on this side of the country, that is to say between Compeign on one side, Cambray on the second, and Dunkirk on the third.

Fame tells us that he did several remarkable exploits on the side of Artois, between Calais and St Omer, and between Pont Oyse and Cambray ; as also between Dunkirk and Ipries, Dunkirk and Boulogne, and the like, and this was confirmed in that he was not much heard off on any other side of the country.

But to come to facts :—one of the most notorious robberies he was immediately concerned in after his coming to Flanders was that of the post between Lisle and Paris, where, it was said, they got a great booty, consisting of gold in specie, with negotiated bills of exchange to a very great amount ; this was said to be an exceeding loss to the merchants of Lisle, besides that it greatly injured the credit of the post, by which bills of exchange accepted were frequently carried with the utmost security, and now lay in the narrow compass of a post-letter.

This would, no question, have been carried on, had not the governor taken care to prevent it, by conveying the post from Lisle by a party of soldiers from one fortified place to another, so that the mails were admitted again to be thoroughly safe.

About September last, having a mind to get a large society of his men together, Le Bizeau comes to Calais, and on an extraordinary occasion. Our author does not assign the particular cause which brought him to Calais, but it seems that he had intelligence of some very great booty, and that he was well assured of it. It was here that he solicited his old servants to come to him, as to one that had formerly always assured them of good purchase when they did ; accordingly he had an unusual assembly about him when at Calais, and sometimes they went one way, and sometimes another ; but it is said a new view offered itself, which made him remove out of Calais for some time, and take up his station at Furnes or Berg St Winox, where they expected the carrying some moidores of Portugal gold from Dunkirk to Lisle ; and this, had it happened, had required a strong gang of fellows, for that the merchants generally take care to have a good guard go along with their gold, though it had always the good fortune to go safe and uninterrupted.

While they remained here, lurking for the return of a spy they had sent to Dunkirk, and by whom they were to be furnished with intelligence, behold a sudden summons calls them out another way, and that, as was supposed, to an easy booty.

I should have taken notice here, that while

they lay about Furnes and St Winox Berg as above, they had certain houses of reception in particular by-places, that is to say, houses of entertainment, which were kept, perhaps, by some of their own gang, or by such as belonged to them, and particularly in the way between Dunkirk and Ipres, they had a house kept by a widow, whose husband, when she had one, was one of the wicked fraternity, and who willingly harboured the whole gang.

This widow received, not only the gang, but even their wives, or whores, or whatever they were called; and these were they, our author says, from whom on several occasions they were whetted on to blood.

It happened, says our author, a little before the fatal exploit of all, that they robbed a company of shop-keepers and tradesmen of Lisle, who not only parted unwillingly with what they had about them, though not much neither, but who gave some fatal descriptions of the robbers, and which they were so well known by, that they were very much perplexed with it, so that, in short, they were very often obliged to change their habits, disguise their faces, shift their horses, and the like.

The women upbraided them, says our author, that had they made clear work, as they called it, with them, that is to say, cut all their throats, they had been safe and out of all danger; and so often did they repeat this bloody doctrine to them, and so home did they press them, that, as it is said, they promised their most Christian wives that they would make surer work of it next time.

In this juncture of time comes the unhappy intelligence, to them, of a set of English gentlemen just come on shore at Calais, who had about three hundred guineas in gold about them, and that they were just preparing to go forward to Paris.

The account was o particular, and the purchase so good, that they embarked for the attempt with the utmost cheerfulness, and the night between the twentieth and twenty-first of September, one thousand seven hundred and twenty-three, they all set out: they posted themselves in a little village near St Inglevret, not far from Boulogne, where they refreshed themselves, and in the morning took the road for Calais.

About four o'clock, according to the intelligence they had received, they met the gentlemen coming forward in two post-chaises, whom they immediately stopped and robbed, for they made no resistance.

Having thus had the booty they expected, they called a council among themselves, what to do with the gentlemen they had robbed; when calling to mind the hellish reproaches of the bloody wretches, their females, they resolved to murder all the gentlemen, with their attendants, and immediately fell upon them, and butchered them, as has been made public to the world. The brief account, as testified by the only surviving person, the servant Spindelow, is as follows:—

On Tuesday, September 10th, about three o'clock in the afternoon, we set out from Calais for Boulogne, in our way to Paris; my master Sebright (the best of masters) and Mr Davies being in one chaise, and Mr Mompesson and myself in another, and his own servant on horseback. About three quarters of a mile beyond the second post, being near seven miles from Calais, we were set upon by six highwaymen, who, having stopped the postilions, came up to the chaises and demanded our money; and the same was readily surrendered to them, for we had no fire-arms with us to make resistance, and even the gentlemen's swords were taken from them. Then taking us out of the chaises, we were all commanded to lie down upon our faces, as were the postilions too, which was presently obeyed; upon which one of the rogues came and rifled our pockets, and narrowly searched the waists and linings of our breeches. This being done, I was ordered to get up and open the portmanteaus; and as I was going to do it, I saw one of them pull the dead body of Mr Lock out of the chaise, in which he had been killed on his return from Paris, at some small distance from us; this was a sad presage of what was like to follow. Mr Lock's servant, who was a Swiss, was spared, but made to lie on his face at the place where they met him. In rifling Mr Sebright's portmanteau, they found some things wrapped up, which they suspected I endeavoured to conceal, which made them cut me with a sword very dangerously in the head. When they had done with my master's portmanteau, they ordered Mr Mompesson to open his, and he desired Mr Sebright to tell them, in French, that his servant was gone before, and had got the key with him. This servant they had met with not far off, and had shot him in the back; but he, not being dead, was ordered to lie down on his face, and now they fetched him to open his master's portmanteau.

When they had finished their search of the portmanteaus and cloak-bags, shaking every piece of linen for fear of missing any money, then the barbarous ruffians gave the word to kill; whereupon one stabbed me in five places in the body, and left me for dead; and with the same sword he struck at Mr Davies several times, and cleft his scull. Who was butchered next, or what immediately followed, I cannot tell, being stunned by one of the villains, who came up to me and stamped three times upon my head, as I was lying upon my face. As soon as I came a little to myself, I perceived by his groans that they were murdering Mr Mompesson, whose throat they cut, and otherwise wounded him; but he survived his wounds for some time.

About that time a peasant that was accidentally passing by was brought in amongst us, and made to lie with his face to the ground, who, perceiving what sort of work they were upon, got up, and attempted to run away, but they rode after him, and shot him dead. After this they visited me once more, and having turned me about, to see if I had any life remaining, but observing none, they left me there weltering in my blood. The bloody scene being then ended, they packed up their booty, carrying away two cloak-bags, filled with the best of the things; and having a horse that was small and poor, they shot him themselves, and took away a better out of one of the chaises in his room.

About a quarter of an hour after they were gone, we heard the peasants talking over the dead bodies, and Mr Mompesson and myself, lifting up our heads as well as we could, perceived they were carrying away what things were left. We desired them to help us into the chaise, but they refused to do it ; so with much difficulty Mr Mompesson got himself in, and I crawled up to it, and got my body in, while my legs hung out, and in that posture we were carried to a little house three quarters of a mile from the place, and one of the peasants was so kind as to lead the chaise : the people of the house brought some straw, and laid us upon it, and there we lay in great misery that night. Mr Mompesson took notice in the night, that he thought the rogues were but indifferently paid for the drudgery of butchering so many (five persons being then murdered, and himself, who died soon after, made the sixth); "for," saith he, "besides watches, rings, linen, &c., they had but one hundred and twenty guineas amongst us all, and the payment of the bills will be stopped at Paris."

Mr Sebright had changed at Calais about twenty-five guineas into silver (not three hundred as was given out) to bear our expenses upon the road. And whereas it was reported that he said to the ruffians—he knew one of them ; which expression is supposed, by some, to have occasioned the sad catastrophe, which it might have done, had it been true, but the said report is absolutely false and groundless, and highly injurious to the memory of that worthy though unfortunate gentleman. The murder was, doubtless, preconcerted among them, and resolved upon ; and they tell us in that country, that some time before a certain company had drank, at a house upon the road, an uncommon quantity of brandy, who are supposed to be this wicked gang, in order to work themselves up to a sufficient rage for the committing of so much barbarity.

Next morning we were carried from our little cottage upon the road back to Calais, where several of the most able surgeons of the place were sent for, to take care of us, and dress our wounds. They sewed up Mr Mompesson's throat, and finding he had a fever, bled him, but he died a few hours after.

Another report was spread here, and transmitted to France, which, in justice to truth and to the injured person, I think myself obliged to contradict, viz., that the woman's son at the Silver Lion Inn at Calais was taken up on suspicion of having a hand in that horrid action, upon which account they have since been great sufferers at that house, but the said report is as false as anything can be true ; on the contrary, those people bear the best of characters.

I have here given you the substance of the report I made more at large to the President at Calais, which he told me he would have printed, and sent to England, when I waited upon him some days before I left that place, to thank him for the great care he had taken in this unhappy affair, and at the same time described to him the features of two of the rogues, who had something remarkable in their faces. What account the postilions gave of the matter, I know not. but it is said to be little, and next to none.

A person was some time since taken up at Lisle, and said to be the old man that was among them, for such there was in the gang ; but, upon his trial, he did not appear to be the same ; however, he was broke on the wheel for a robbery committed by him about four years ago.

We hear of another person taken up near Boulogne, who is in gaol there on account of some words that he spoke, as it is said, in a drunken frolic, so that it is much doubted that he was a party concerned, though he hath got a stone doublet by the bargain ; but it is to be hoped that the perpetrators of so much wickedness will be apprehended, and in that case, I expect to be sent for to France, and if so, you shall hear farther from

Your humble servant,

R. SPINDELOW.

This inhuman butchery soon spread its fame over the whole country ; and as it filled the ears of all that heard it with horror, so the search after the murderers was so sudden, so strict, and so general, that it forced them all to leave even the closest retreats they had, and to fly the country.

Bizeau, in particular, took to his old retreat, says our author, and went up into Lorrain, where he had been before, and where he was not to seek of his lurking holes and receivers, in which he had formerly been harboured.

Yet, even here, he found the fame of the murder committed on the English gentlemen had reached the ears of the people ; the whole society of mankind seemed to be alarmed, and the general search after all suspected, loose, or vagrant persons, was very strict, and several such were taken up, among which, and that increased their fears, were two who were really in the secret of the murder, though not in the fact, and by whose being examined some light was gained into the persons who were really guilty.

This, no doubt, made Bizeau and Le Febvre often shift their dens and fly from one place to another, as being in continual uneasiness and apprehensions of being discovered. They would have fled farther off, but they perceived, let them go where they would, it would be the same ; for that, as before, the Court of France had written, in the most pressing terms, to all the neighbouring princes to intercept strangers, especially French, and cause them to be most strictly examined.

The consternation they were in on this occasion must be very great, and they quitted their old quarters in Lorrain, and, says he, came down into the low countries, and particularly took up their stand in Walloon Flanders, at or about Valenciennes.

Here they changed their names, and Bizeau, in particular, called himself Gratien Devanelle, a Walloon, and gave himself out to be a working silversmith and jeweller, and carried about him the proper tools of that trade, though he understood little or nothing of it.

Their disguise served them but too well, and they were so effectually concealed by it that they got harbour in several houses, where they were not at all suspected about Conde. Hence they removed to Lisle, where, pretending the same trade, and being recommended by people of credit from their former quarters, where it seems they had behaved civilly, they were easily received at Lisle also; nor was it hard to be entertained at a second place, when they had a fair testimonial, or certification, from the first.

Here they got separate lodgings, and seemed not to correspond or be acquainted with one another; but, having each of them a wife with him, put on the face of artificers in appearance, working diligently at their trades; keeping, however, a strict secret intelligence one with another all the while for the carrying on their wicked private business, which they never quitted.

In this place they seemed now to have gotten a kind of settlement, and to have escaped all the dangers of a discovery; and perhaps, had they been able to have restrained themselves from the old trade of thieving, they might have gone on undiscovered to this day, but two things broke in upon their repose. 1. They understood here that the two fellows who were taken up at Nancy in Lorrain had pretended, on examination, to know something of the robbers who murdered the English gentlemen, and to give some description of them, their persons, their places of retreat, and employment, though it was too imperfect an account to guide the officers of justice to an inquiry.

This 'tis probable they had intelligence of from some of their gang, who yet lay undiscovered in that country; to which was added, that several places where they had been concealed had been searched, and the people taken up on suspicion; and that it was likely they would be put to the torture to make them confess who it was they had so entertained, and what other haunts they had, where they might be inquired after; but as it happened they had not communicated that part to any of those people, so they could give no account of them, if they were tortured; no, not to save their lives.

Though these strict inquiries made them anxious, yet it did not at all take them off from the practice of their usual villanies; and they made, says our author, many successful sallies in private, some one way and some another; sometimes together, and sometimes apart; by which they supported their expense, and yet managed with such dexterity that they always escaped pursuit, and for some time so much as being suspected.

Nor, perhaps, had these two capital rogues been suspected at all, if, on the strict searches that were made upon the news of the murder of the English gentlemen, several lesser rogues had not fallen into the hands of justice, who, though engaged only in a kind of inferior villanies, and so not concerned with these in the bloody and cruel attempts they were generally employed in, yet knew of them, and upon their examination gave such accounts of them as that by these means the officers of the Lieutenant General de Police came to know that there was such a gang, and perhaps to know some of their haunts, and, consequently, a stricter search was made after them than had ever been done before; nor, when these accounts were given of them, was it any longer doubted but that these were the men that had committed the barbarous massacre of the English gentlemen between Calais and Boulogne.

After the government had thus gotten a scent of them, they were put more to their shifts to conceal themselves, and they quitted their old habitations and retreats, and though it was difficult, yet they did so effectually manage, that they not only escaped, but had the boldness still to continue their horrid trade, as well of murder as of robbery.

In consequence of this desperate boldness, they attacked the Lisle stage-coach about two months after the robbery of the English gentlemen. In this adventure they were both concerned, as they had been in the other.

They, it seems, had received some private intelligence of a great sum of money which was to be carried in the coach that time from Lisle to Paris, and that there would be six or eight men on horseback well armed to guard it, notwithstanding which, they resolved to attack them, and carry off the money or die in the attempt. To this purpose, they were no less than ten in number when they set out; but, upon better intelligence, and that there were no more than two servants attending the coach, they separated, and only five went forward on the design of robbing the coach, and the other five went towards Roan on some other scent, believing, that seeing the number of horsemen were reduced to only two instead of eight, so the treasure was also left behind, perhaps for that week only. They waited for the coach on the road between Peronne on the River Somme and the little town of Bapaume, where, taking a convenient post on the edge of the wood, they stopped the postilion, firing a pistol at him, which missing the fellow, hurt one of the horses only. The two horsemen behaved very well, but were both murdered, and the passengers put into the utmost terror and consternation, expecting they should be all murdered also. The names of the two men on horseback were John Pouillard and Lawrence Hennelet, servants.

Having thus cleared the field, as it might be said, of their opposers, they robbed the coach, in which our author says they used the passengers very rudely and barbarously, and two ladies especially, who they wounded in getting rings from their fingers, besides other indecencies and cruelties not to be named, and were, but with the most humble and passionate entreaties, prevailed with to save their lives; indeed, considering how they had been flushed with blood for some time past, it was a wonder they had not killed them all.

Our author does not give any account of what booty they took on this occasion, only adds, that this was the last of their villanies; that now the days of their account began to come on, for that, within a few days after this robbery, the coachman and passengers having given the best description of them that they were able to do of men in masks, for so, it seems, they were at that time, though not when they attacked the English gentlemen. We say, the description being given as well as it could be in such circumstances, the two principals, namely, Bizeau, then called Davanelle, and Peter le Febvre, were taken up at Lisle upon suspicion; the other Bizeau and three more, who were in the fact, escaped for that time.

Being thus in the hands of justice, rather on suspicion of robbery than on any positive evidence of the fact, the more general inquiry was directed to the murder of the English gentlemen. They denied it stiffly, but yet all their answers seemed to be studied and uncertain, faltering and shuffling; sometimes they were in Switzerland at that time, another time they were at Paris, another time sick, and thus their very denial rather increased than abated the suspicions of their guilt.

Upon all these inquiries, the Lieutenant General de Police thought fit to have them brought to Paris, where they went more seriously to work with them, and had them examined upon all the particulars apart, and as they were kept asunder, and not permitted to see the confession that either had separately made, they began to suspect one another, each one doubting that the other should impeach him of the fact, to obtain his own pardon.

But neither did this produce a full confession, though it gave sufficient light to convince the Judges Criminal that they were the men, while they had not yet such positive proof of it as was sufficient to convict and attaint them.

Upon this occasion it was that they sent over to England to desire that Richard Spindelow, the servant to Mr Sebright, might be sent over to give evidence in the case as to the persons of the men, and the particulars of the murder, which, our author says, he accordingly did.

This Spindelow was, they supposed, murdered with the rest; nay, they turned and rolled him about after a great interval of his wounds, and finding no breath in him, as they believed, they left him as a dead corpse; yet he afterwards recovered.

His evidence, together with their confused, faltering answers, were, it's said, found sufficient by the Judges Criminal, to declare these two guilty, both of the murder and robbery; the trials in France being not by juries as in England, but by the judgment of the court, or bench of judges, and these, we say, with one voice, pronounced them guilty, as well of the robbery and murder of the English gentlemen, as also of the robbery of the Lisle coach, and the murder of the two servants that attended it.

Bizeau behaved till now with an obdurate kind of bravery, and Le Febvre with stupidity of mind—both insensible of their condition—nor could the fathers, who were admitted to attend them, prevail with them to make any serious reflections, or so much as to suppose they were in any circumstance which required such reflections.

But when they found they were condemned, and that they saw death at the door, that it was unavoidable, nor any delay of the execution to be obtained, they began both of them, but especially Bizeau, to relent, and look with the countenance of guilty criminals. The sentence pronounced, as our author gives it us from the forms of their justice, is thus:—

EXTRACT from the Register of the Court of Justice, held for the Chatelet of Paris.

" An accusation being pursued, at the instance of the king's procurator-general, against Joseph Bizeau, who had taken upon himself the name of Gratien Devanelle, jeweller, of the city of Liege, and Peter Le Febvre, also jeweller; Elizabeth Gottequin, wife of the said Le Febvre; Mary Merance, wife of Francis Nicholas Josette, a seller of Indian goods; John Baptist Bizeau, toyman; Andrian Beausse, vintner; Catherine Moffet, wife of the said Adrian Beausse, and Mary Beausse, their daughter; Anne Turry, wife of Francis Puget, alias Farcinet; Mary Catherine Francois, alias Catherine Cantas, and Mary Frances Beausse, widow of Francis Caron, vintner, at Beauval, defendants, and accused.

" The court declared that the aforesaid Joseph Bizeau alias Gratien Devanelle, and Peter Le Febvre, were duly attainted and convicted of the robberies and assassinations committed upon the persons of the English gentlemen and their servants, named Lock, Sebright, Mompesson, Davies, Fitzgerald, and Richard Spindelow, and also one named Allet and Lewis Poilet, upon the high road to Boulogne, between Brighen and St Ingleverd, the 21st of September last; and also of the robbery of the stage coach belonging to Lisle, with armed force upon the high road near the village of Mazincourt, two leagues and a half from Peronne, the 19th of November last; and of the assassination, committed at the same time, upon the persons of John Pouillard and Lawrence Hennelet, who accompanied the said coach. In atonement, therefore, for the crimes mentioned as aforesaid, and in regard to justice, the said Joseph Bizeau, alias Gratien Devanelle, and Peter Le Febvre, are condemned to have their arms, legs, thighs, &c., broken upon a scaffold, which shall be erected for that purpose at the common place of execution in the city of Paris; after which said execution their bodies shall be put upon wheels, with their faces towards the sky, there to remain for so much time, and as long as it shall please God to continue them alive. The goods acquired by them are confiscated to the king, or to whom they shall be found to appertain, save one thousand livres, which shall be taken out of what belongs to each of them, to cause prayers to be offered up to implore God for the repose of the souls of the several persons aforementioned whom they have assassinated, and the same sum of one thousand livres out of each of their effects, as fines to the king, in case the profit arising by confiscation do not accrue to his majesty; and farther, that before execution the said Joseph Bizeau alias Gratien Devanelle, and Peter Le Febvre shall be put to the question (torture), ordinary and extraordinary, to the end that the truth of the facts resulting from their trial, as well as the names of their accomplices, may be known from their own mouths. The dead bodies, viz., that of Joseph Bizeau alias Gratien Devanelle, to be carried and remain exposed on a wheel, upon the high road to Calais, and that of Peter Le Febvre to be exposed after the same manner upon the high road to Peronne.

" The court was farther pleased to order, that sentence against John Baptist Bizeau, Elizabeth Gottequin, Mary Merance, Adrian Beausse, Catherine Moffet, Mary Beausse, Anne Turry, Mary Catherine Francois alias Catherine Cantas, and Mary Jean Beausse, should be suspended till after the execution of the present sentence; and the court further directed that the warrant issued out for the taking John Baptist Le Febvre, Lamant, Dupuis, Josette, Lewis Le Febvre, and three women, who passed for the wives of the said Lamant, John Baptist Le Febvre, and Lewis Le Febvre, should be put in execution, according to the indications the court hath received; and that an accusation be drawn up against them, that they may be proceeded against according to the utmost rigour of the law. Given Thursday the 13th of July, N.S., 1724.

"Signed,   Caillet Greffier of the Court.

"The sentence of the court was accordingly executed, the 14th of July, N.S., upon the aforesaid Joseph Bizeau *alias* Gratien Devanelle, and Peter Le Febvre, with the utmost severity, they being left to expire in their torment, without obtaining the ordinary dispatch, called the *coup de grace*. All this is done as well in justice to the English nation, for the inhuman murder of the gentlemen above-mentioned, as for the other assassinations and crimes they were found guilty of, as appears from the foregoing proceedings."

When they had it read to them, and that they were appointed to be tortured also before execution, they made bitter lamentations and expostulations, kneeling to the judges for mercy; but were told, that they had nothing to do but to kneel to God and the blessed Virgin, for that no mercy could be expected here, where their crimes had been so atrocious and so horrid, that no Christian's ears could hear them without horror and astonishment.

The same day in which they received sentence they were put to the question, that is to say, were tortured upon the rack, where they fully confessed both the robberies and murders above mentioned, namely, that of the English gentlemen, with the peasant who was passing by, and that of the Lisle coach, with the murder of the two horsemen attending it; so that by their own confession they were justly put to death.

They were interrogated also concerning the other robberies and murders which they had been guilty of, and they confessed so many, says our author, that it was horrible to hear that two such execrable wretches should have been so let loose upon mankind, to commit so many murders and villanies.

They passed the time, the night before their execution, in the prison for the dead, as called there (or condemned hold, as in England) with strange, uncouth cries and groanings; occasioned, says he, partly by the pains of their tortured joints, but much more by the torture of their souls; the fathers appointed to attend them in vain administering to them their pious exhortations to repentance, and comforting them, as well as possible, in so dismal a condition.

On the morrow, being the 14th, Bizeau was led out to the greve to execution, all the way calling on the people to pray for him, and showing great marks of penitence, which continued to the last. He was broke alive, in the extremest sense, not being allowed the *coup de grace*, and lived many hours on the wheel, being not expired many hours before Le Febvre was brought to the same place, nay, our author hints, that he understood by some that he was not quite dead when Le Febvre came to execution, which must be at least twenty-four hours.

It was thought fit to allow the executioner leave to give the *coup de grace* to the latter, as is usual, so that he died with less torment than the other.

Thus perished these two execrable wretches, and as there are five more who are in the prison of the Conciergerie, and eight more who are not yet taken, we expect more executions on the same occasion.